AMAZING PLACES

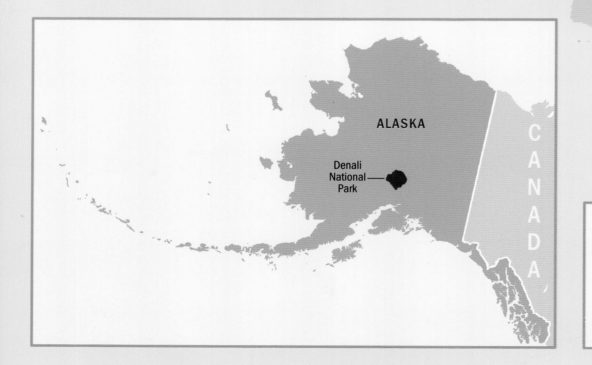

UNITED S

CALIFORNIA

● —Chinatown

Grand
Canyon
National
Park

ARIZONA

ALASKA

Denali
National —●
Park

CANADA

MEXICO

CANADA

TES

WISCONSIN
Oneida
Nation
Museum

Niagara
Falls

NEW
YORK

Fenway
Park

MASSACHUSETTS

PENNSYLVANIA

Harlem

Sandy Hook
Lighthouse

Liberty
Bell

NEW
JERSEY

WASHINGTON, DC
National
Museum of the
American Indian

KANSAS
Watkins
Museum
of History

Mississippi
River

State Fair
of Texas

MISSISSIPPI

FLORIDA

TEXAS

The Ringling
Circus Museum

N

W   E

S

To Renée M. LaTulippe—
who has taken me
to amazing places
of poetry —L.B.H.

For CJ and Crystal, my future travelers. Your
wonderment at the simplest things puts a smile
in my heart. I hope to discover many of these
amazing places with you. Your happiness will
always be mine. Daddy. —C.S.

In memory of my father, Harold Charles Hale,
and our cross-country car trips to amazing places —C.H.

Acknowledgments
Thanks are due to the following for use of works in this collection: Curtis Brown, Ltd. for "Midway Magic" by Rebecca Kai Dotlich. Copyright © 2015 by Rebecca Kai Dotlich; "Tree Speaks" by Nikki Grimes. Copyright © 2015 by Nikki Grimes; "Langston" by Lee Bennett Hopkins. Copyright © 2015 by Lee Bennett Hopkins; "Niagara" by Prince Redcloud. Copyright © 2015 by Prince Redcloud. All used by permission of Curtis Brown, Ltd. All other works are used by permission of the respective poets, who control all rights; all copyright © 2015: Alma Flor Ada for "A Sunday Trip to Chinatown"; Jaime Adoff for "1 2 5"; Joseph Bruchac for "Longhouse Song"; Kristine O'Connell George for "The Moccasins"; Joan Bransfield Graham for "Sandy Hook Lighthouse"; J. Patrick Lewis for "On the Mississippi"; Jane Medina for "Runaway"; Linda Sue Park for "Bell"; Charles Waters for "Fenway Park"; Janet S. Wong for "Campfire."

Thanks also to Alice Adamczyk, independent researcher and retired librarian, Schomburg Center for Research in Black Culture; Kraig Anderson, LighthouseFriends.com; Joseph Bruchac (Abenaki), Doug George/Kanentiio (Mohawk), and Bill Loran (Mohawk); Fenway Ambassador Phil Derick and staff, Boston Red Sox; Doris Fanelli, PhD, Chief of Division of Cultural Resources Management, Independence National Historical Park; Kris Fister, Public Affairs Officer, Denali National Park and Preserve; Matthew Lew, Resource Development Assistant, and colleagues, (SF) Chinatown Community Development Center; Edward M. McClure, librarian, Grand Canyon National Park Research Library; Mississippi National River and Recreation Area, National Park Service; Steve Nowak, Executive Director, Douglas County (KS) Historical Society; Jennifer Lemmer Posey, Assistant Curator of the Circus Museum, The John and Mable Ringling Museum of Art; and State Fair of Texas Public Relations Department for their valuable assistance reviewing material in the book.

Collection copyright © 2015 by Lee Bennett Hopkins
Illustrations copyright © 2015 by Chris Soentpiet and Christy Hale
LEE & LOW BOOKS Inc., 95 Madison Avenue, New York, NY 10016, leeandlow.com
Book design by Christy Hale
Book production by The Kids at Our House
The text is set in ITC Franklin Gothic Book
The illustrations are rendered in pencil and colored digitally
Manufactured in China by Jade Productions, January 2018
Printed on paper from responsible sources
(hc) 10 9 8 7 6 5 4 3 2 1
(pb) 10 9 8 7 6 5 4 3 2 1
First edition

Library of Congress Cataloging-in-Publication Data
Amazing places : poems / selected by Lee Bennett Hopkins ; illustrations by Chris Soentpiet and Christy Hale. — First edition.
    pages cm
ISBN 978-1-60060-653-3 (hardcover) ISBN 978-1-62014-805-1 (paperback)
1. Geography—Juvenile poetry. 2. Historic sites—Juvenile poetry. 3. Children's poetry, American. I. Hopkins, Lee Bennett, editor. II. Soentpiet, Chris K., illustrator. III. Hale, Christy, illustrator.
PS595.G4A43 2015   811.008'032—dc23   2015009199

AMAZING PLACES

POEMS SELECTED BY LEE BENNETT HOPKINS

ILLUSTRATIONS BY CHRIS SOENTPIET & CHRISTY HALE

Lee & Low Books Inc. • New York

CAMPFIRE

Just think—
when Mother was my age,
she could build a fire
with sparks from rocks,
catch a bunch of
grasshoppers and
roast them whole
for a summer
night's snack!

"Get me a good stick,"
she says, "thin but strong,"
and I bring her one
from the woods
behind our tent.
On the way back
I see a brown bag
by her feet—
could it be?

When the fire is spitting ready,
she reaches
in the bag, rustling,
and hands me
one big, fat, luscious
marshmallow.

JANET S. WONG

DENALI NATIONAL PARK, *Alaska*

LONGHOUSE SONG

When I bend down to enter into the longhouse
my sons and I made this spring
up in my grandfather's field—
where the hooves of horses,
the sharp blades of plows,
and the throb of a tractor's heartless breath
once replaced an older way of seeing
and staying close to the listening land—
it seems I can begin again, begin to hear this song:

Elm bark is my skin,
bent saplings my bones,
my mouth that draws
in the living wind
is the door to the coming of sun.

My breath
is the smoke
rising up to join sky.
My heart is the fire
in the circle of stones.

My eyes, my spirit,
and my thoughts
belong to you,
whose human dreams
kept close to the earth
will always be held
in Creation's embrace
through the memoried
circles of seasons.

JOSEPH BRUCHAC

ONEIDA NATION MUSEUM, *near Green Bay, Wisconsin*

LANGSTON

Who would have known
a young lad
delivering
door-to-door newspapers
in a small town
would one day
see people the world over
carrying *his* papers—

his reams of poems—

poems about—

rainy sidewalks,
stormy seas,
crystal stair memories,
moon-glimmers,
moonbeams,
but best of all,

      his dusts of dreams.

LEE BENNETT HOPKINS

WATKINS MUSEUM OF HISTORY, *Lawrence, Kansas*

A SUNDAY TRIP TO CHINATOWN

Today in Chinatown
Dad offers each of us a treat.
"Mine is this meal," he says,
while we choose
favorite dishes from the dim sum cart.

We move slowly on crowded sidewalks
admiring shop windows
with all sorts of wonders.
Roberto knows his wish:
firecrackers for the Fourth of July.

My mother quietly chooses
a jade bracelet,
winking at my sister.
Mamá's treat will become a present
for Julia's *quinceañera*.

Julia brings a chime
of small bronze shells.
"It will look nice in your garden."
My mother's face lights up.
Julia's choice: a way of saying thanks.

And for me?
I've already had so many treats this morning:
  the flavors of the food
  the smell of incense sticks
  the colors all around us
  and best of all—the sounds.

Listening to the clipped singing tones
of people's speech
I give myself my own gift—
the promise
that I will learn
to speak Chinese.

Alma Flor Ada

quinceañera (keen-seh-ah-NYAI-rah): girl's fifteenth-birthday celebration

CHINATOWN, *San Francisco, California*

TREE SPEAKS

Here they come again
those pale, rootless humans
squinting at the far country
where gorge meets sky.
How they gawk at me,
thinking I'm lonely!
Yes, I am one of only
a handful of trees
clinging to these
sun-striped cliffs,
branches suspended
over a clear drop
more miles down
than the number of rings
circling my middle.
But lonely?
What do they know?
Daily, I listen to the echo
of the Colorado River rapids
bouncing off red-purple ridges
sculpted by water and time.
Each morning,
I witness the swoop and swirl
of hawks dancing in the air
we share.

Each evening,
I happily offer my limbs
as respite for majestic eagles.
Oh, yes,
this home of mine
stitched to the horizon
is Grand.
I will cling here forever,
waiting to be found
by those lost
in the endless beauty
of the Canyon.

NIKKI GRIMES

GRAND CANYON NATIONAL PARK, *Arizona*

MIDWAY MAGIC

A Ferris wheel spins
waterfalling with lights,
magicians toss magic
to warm, wild nights.

Summer air sings
with flurries of fun,
bright bubbling colors
all rolled into one.

Swirling and twirling
beneath sparkling stars,
in pink Teacups,
in Bumper cars.

A clanging of coasters,
seats dangling midair,
such rumbles and tumbles—

Call it:

   STATE FAIR

R<small>EBECCA</small> K<small>AI</small> D<small>OTLICH</small>

STATE FAIR OF TEXAS, *Dallas, Texas*

ON THE MISSISSIPPI

Down along the Great River Road,
A barge takes aim and hauls its load

To quiet village or old mill town,
The way long since gone gray or brown.

From St. Louis on to New Orleans,
Bright pictures of American scenes

Are hung behind each lock and dam—
The mural painter? Uncle Sam.

No matter that water eddies, churns,
Or has become becalmed by turns,

The ample barge follows its nose,
Making a magic as it goes.

Once the giant rounds the bend,
My friend and I will play pretend,

Looking upriver—what will it bring?—
Waiting to see the next big thing.

J. Patrick Lewis

MISSISSIPPI RIVER, *Mississippi*

RUNAWAY

I'm running away to where people can fly:
they flip, twist,
and twirl
as they break through sky.

I'm running away to where animals dance:
seals in top hats,
dogs in short pants.

I'm running away where it's okay to laugh
at pratfalls and magic
or ragged riffraff.

I'm running away where the world is a tent:
each day
an adventure,
each night an event.

I'm running away with people who fly,
I'll dance and
I'll laugh
and forget how to cry.

Jane Medina

THE RINGLING CIRCUS MUSEUM, *Sarasota, Florida*

Bell

1753

Maybe there was a boy
who fetched tools for weeks,
watched whenever he could,
then held the reins steady
so it could be loaded onto the cart
and waved as it was hauled away.

1776

Did it ring that day in July?
No one knows for sure now.
But maybe there was a girl
who was putting away her broom
after sweeping the statehouse
who lifted her head to listen
as it rang time after time,
each bong vibrating through her body,
the sound so strong she could lean on it.

1846

Maybe it was a child who noticed first,
before any of the grown-ups did,
who cocked an ear and frowned
as the pure clear peal crumbled,
and a crack crazed its way to fame.

1915

Maybe there was a brother and a sister
who saw it in Indiana, or Oklahoma,
or Oregon, on its cross-country tour
who were lifted onto the platform
so they could touch its side
warm from the sun, and trace
the zigzag with a fingertip.

Today/Tomorrow

Maybe there is a girl or a boy
who can hear the echo in the silence,
who can see the past in the present,
and imagine what is not but should be,
and grow up to make it so.

LINDA SUE PARK

LIBERTY BELL, *Philadelphia, Pennsylvania*

THE MOCCASINS

A pair of tiny moccasins
standing in a neat straight line,
standing quietly behind glass.
On display, a child's small shoes,
buffalo hide, beaten soft,
faded brown, a whisper of dust.

Once, one fell off when she ran;
she tucked them under her arm
when she waded in the stream.
She curled her toes up inside
when she crouched to see what was
inside a ground squirrel's hole.

Watch for her tonight—tiptoe—
across the cold tile—open—
the glass display case—reclaim
her shoes. Watch for her tonight,
running, running soundlessly
into the moonlight, leaving
no footprints.

KRISTINE O'CONNELL GEORGE

NATIONAL MUSEUM OF THE AMERICAN INDIAN, *Washington, DC*

SANDY HOOK LIGHTHOUSE

Wild
storms rage,
lightning crackles,
n o t h i n g
deters me.
I h a v e
s t o o d on
duty in this
place for
over two
centuries.
Sentinel
of the sea,
I battle
darkness,
pierce it
with sabers
of l i g h t,
warn you
away from
treacherous
s h o a l s . . .
determined
to protect you,
welcome you to
New York Harbor,
keep you S A F E.
**SANDY HOOK
LIGHTHOUSE**

JOAN BRANSFIELD GRAHAM

SANDY HOOK LIGHTHOUSE, *Fort Hancock, New Jersey*

125

One-twenty-fifth opens into a w i d e grin

s m i l i n g

as me and Grandma Wren
take our Saturday afternoon walk.
Harlem hops, pops,
rocks and rolls on waves of folks
doin' what they do.
Goin' here and there—
We pass Ms. Claire's *everything you could ever need store.*
And then the WORLD FAMOUS A P O L L O . . .
Passing a juice bar, and an African bazaar—
I can tell we're getting close.

Shut my eyes—see him flyin' down the court.
He shoots—he scores!

"We're here," Grandma Wren says.
"Magic Johnson movie theater."

She gives me a squeeze as we walk inside.
I leave my friend One-twenty-five
to keep on keepin' on—

Don't miss me too much while I'm gone.

JAIME ADOFF

HARLEM, *New York City, New York*

FENWAY PARK

In Major League's oldest
baseball park
Red Sox Nation
provides a spark.

Its brick veneer
holds a diamond within.
We hurry inside.
Game's about to begin.

While we sip clam chowder
on a crisp, fall night,
we cheer as a ball
takes off in flight.

I high-five Grandpa:
a double play!

Fenway—

a tradition
that will never go away.

CHARLES WATERS

FENWAY PARK, *Boston, Massachusetts*

NIAGARA

falls
    and
        falls
forever-ever
        flowing

falling
falling

cascading
crashing
dipping
dropping
plunging
tumbling

        stop

hear
    ancestral voices
        cry

        Onguiaahra
        Onguiaahra

Thunder of Waters

        Onguiaahra
        Onguiaahra

forever   *On-gui-aah-ra*

Prince Redcloud

Onguiaahra (own-gwee-ah-lah): Seneca word that has been translated as
  "Thunder of Waters"; often said to be the source of the name Niagara

NIAGARA FALLS, *Niagara Falls, New York*

MORE ABOUT THE AMAZING PLACES

CAMPFIRE
DENALI NATIONAL PARK, *Alaska*

Established in 1917 as Mount McKinley National Park, Denali was the world's first national park created to protect wildlife. The park covers about 6 million acres (2.4 million hectares) of land and is home to a diversity of mammals, birds, fish, and plants. Today more than five hundred thousand people visit the park each year; and seeing bears, caribou, and other Alaskan wildlife in the midst of incredibly beautiful landscapes is part of the Denali experience. When it is not too cloudy, visitors may be able to view Denali (also known as Mount McKinley), which at 20,320 feet (6,194 meters) is the highest mountain peak in North America. Around one thousand mountain climbers come to the park each year to climb to the summit, a once-in-a-lifetime experience.

LONGHOUSE SONG
ONEIDA NATION MUSEUM,
near Green Bay, Wisconsin

A longhouse was a shelter used through the early part of the 1800s by people of the five original Iroquois Nations, of which the Oneida were one. A typical longhouse had a framework of stripped saplings that was covered with elm bark. A large longhouse measured as much as 300 feet (91 meters) long, 50 to 60 feet (15 to 18 meters) wide, and 30 feet (9 meters) tall, and housed twelve or more families, usually of the same clan. The number of families was indicated by the number of smoke holes in the roof. A few miles from Green Bay, Wisconsin, outside the Oneida Nation Museum, stands a replica of a longhouse. Inside the museum, in a smaller replica longhouse, visitors are encouraged to handle the wooden utensils, musical instruments, animal skins, clothing, and other traditional items on display.

LANGSTON
WATKINS MUSEUM OF HISTORY,
Lawrence, Kansas

Langston Hughes (1902–1967), beloved poet, playwright, and novelist, lived in Lawrence, Kansas, from 1903 until 1915. Although he was there for only twelve years, the city has recognized his contributions to literature in several ways. In 1975, a statue was installed at the Watkins Museum of History showing a young Hughes delivering newspapers and carrying a book by scholar and civil rights activist W. E. B. Du Bois. A visiting professorship in Hughes's name was established at the University of Kansas in 1977. In 1980, a plaque with the first line of his poem "Youth" was placed at the entry to city hall. Today, Hughes's birthday, February 1, is marked by the announcement of the winners of the annual Langston Hughes Creative Writing Award, which is sponsored by the Lawrence Arts Center.

A SUNDAY TRIP TO CHINATOWN
CHINATOWN, *San Francisco, California*

San Francisco's Chinatown is the largest Chinese community outside of Asia and the oldest Chinatown in North America. Established in 1848, Chinatown is still an active center of Chinese culture and traditions and is one of the top attractions for visitors to the city. Located in downtown San Francisco, the neighborhood is entered through the Gateway Arch (Dragon Gate), a pagoda-style structure with sculptures of dragons, fish, and two elaborately-carved lions. Portsmouth Square, known as the Heart of Chinatown, is a popular outdoor spot for residents to socialize. While wandering the crowded and noisy streets of Chinatown, visitors encounter people practicing traditional crafts, children playing in alleyways, authentic food markets, busy restaurants, herbal shops, and a variety of other stores selling a wide array of inexpensive trinkets as well as more expensive items.

TREE SPEAKS
GRAND CANYON NATIONAL PARK, *Arizona*

Established in 1919, Grand Canyon National Park is one of the most important geologic areas in the world, containing rocks and fossils that date back billions of years. The park covers 1.2 million acres (485,623 hectares), and close to five million people visit the 1-mile- (1.6-kilometer-) deep canyon each year. In addition to breathtaking rock formations, there are approximately two hundred species of trees and shrubs in the park, among them ponderosa pine, five species of juniper, and quaking aspen. Ravens, hawks, California condors, ospreys, and peregrine falcons are among the hundreds of bird species in the canyon region. The mighty Colorado River that runs through the canyon is home to eight native fish species, while the river's rapids offer thrills for whitewater rafters.

MIDWAY MAGIC
STATE FAIR OF TEXAS, *Dallas, Texas*

The State Fair of Texas, founded in 1886, is one of the largest state fairs in the United States, attracting more than three million visitors to Dallas each year. The fair runs for twenty-four days, starting in late September. Attractions include pig races, mock rodeo events where children ride stick horses, marching bands, livestock exhibits and events, an auto show, shops, and unique foods. The midway features numerous games and more than seventy rides, including a 1914 carousel and a 212-foot- (65-meter-) tall Ferris wheel. The fair's mascot, Big Tex, a huge cowboy figure, has welcomed visitors since 1952. It was destroyed in a fire in October 2012 but was restored in time for the opening of the 2013 season.

Big Tex® is a registered trademark of the State Fair of Texas, and used here by permission.

ON THE MISSISSIPPI
MISSISSIPPI RIVER, *Mississippi*

The Mississippi River is one of North America's longest rivers. It flows for approximately 2,350 miles (3,782 kilometers) from its source at Lake Itasca in northwestern Minnesota south to the Gulf of Mexico just below New Orleans, Louisiana. The famous writer Mark Twain (1835–1910) wrote several stories related to or that are set on the Mississippi. The river is also an important transportation and shipping waterway, with a significant amount of the nation's agricultural products produced in the Mississippi River Basin. These products, plus petroleum, coal, chemical products, sand, gravel, stone, and more are shipped along the Mississippi on boats and barges upriver to US markets or to the port in New Orleans for transporting overseas.

RUNAWAY
THE RINGLING CIRCUS MUSEUM, *Sarasota, Florida*

The Ringling Circus Museum, the first museum in the United States to celebrate the history of all aspects of circus life, was established in 1948. On view are posters, costumes, parade wagons, a cannon, and many other props and equipment used by circus performers. A highlight of the museum is The Howard Bros.

Circus Model, a miniature circus representing Ringling Bros. and Barnum & Bailey Circus shows from 1919 to 1938. Begun more than fifty years ago, pieces are still being added to the one-sixteenth scale model of a three-ring circus. It consists of more than 42,000 items, including a 59-car train, 152 wagons, 8 main tents, more than 800 animals, 1,300 workers and performers, and 7,000 folding chairs. This must-see miniature circus has been delighting visitors of all ages since it was installed in 2006.

BELL
LIBERTY BELL, *Philadelphia, Pennsylvania*

The bell was originally installed in the Pennsylvania State House (now Independence Hall) in 1753, and over the next ninety-three years it was rung for various important events, people, and governmental acts. In the 1830s, the bell was adopted as a symbol of liberty by abolitionists fighting to end slavery, and eventually it became known as the Liberty Bell. No one knows for sure when the bell first cracked, but an attempt to repair the crack by widening it failed when the bell was rung (for the last time) on George Washington's birthday in February 1846. The bell weighs 2,080 pounds (944 kilograms) and is made mostly of copper (70 percent) and tin (25 percent). Since 2003 it has been housed at the Liberty Bell Center in Philadelphia.

THE MOCCASINS
NATIONAL MUSEUM OF THE AMERICAN INDIAN, *Washington, DC*

Established in 1989, the National Museum of the American Indian is dedicated to the preservation, study, understanding, and exhibition of Native cultures of the Western Hemisphere. The building in Washington, DC, which opened in 2004, features architecture, landscaping, and exhibitions designed in collaboration with Native peoples from across the hemisphere. Extensive, diverse collections contain more than eight hundred thousand items representing more than twelve thousand years of history. These include works of historical and religious significance plus items of everyday use, such as weapons, cooking utensils, home items, and clothing, among them carefully sewn moccasins made of soft leather, such as deerskin or beaten buffalo hide. The museum also offers performances, lectures, educational programs, and family events.

SANDY HOOK LIGHTHOUSE

SANDY HOOK LIGHTHOUSE,

Fort Hancock, New Jersey

The Sandy Hook Lighthouse is the oldest standing lighthouse and the oldest operating lighthouse in the United States. Its lamp, which was first lit in 1764, originally burned whale oil but was converted to incandescent electric lights in 1896. Today it is lit by a 1,000-watt bulb magnified through prisms that beam the light 19 nautical miles (22 miles or 35 kilometers) out to sea. The 88-foot- (26.8-meter-) tall lighthouse was built to guide ships safely into and out of New York Harbor, where the tower's thick stone walls protected it from cannon fire during the Revolutionary War. Now surrounded by Fort Hancock, the Sandy Hook Lighthouse was designated a National Historic Landmark in 1964, the year of its two hundredth anniversary.

1 2 5

HARLEM, *New York City, New York*

For more than two hundred years, 125th Street in upper Manhattan, New York City, has been a major crosstown route, passing through the Harlem neighborhood. In the early 1900s, African Americans began moving into Harlem; and ever since 125th Street has been the main thoroughfare of the bustling neighborhood, which is still a major residential and cultural center for African Americans. The street, which has a vibrant rhythm and energy all its own, is home to the world-famous Apollo Theater, where scores of performers of yesterday and today have gotten their starts. A host of large and small shops, restaurants, and markets also line the street. And nearby is a Magic Johnson movie theater complex, named for former Los Angeles Lakers basketball star Earvin "Magic" Johnson Jr.

FENWAY PARK

FENWAY PARK, *Boston, Massachusetts*

Fenway Park, home of the Boston Red Sox since 1912, is the oldest Major League baseball park in the United States, earning it the nickname of America's Most Beloved Ballpark. The stadium can seat approximately 37,000 people at day games and 37,500 at night games, making it also one of the smallest ballparks in the country. Fenway is known for the Green Monster, its 37-foot, 2-inch- (11.3-meter-) tall green left-field wall. About three million people attend Red Sox games at Fenway each year, and the team has won the World Series eight times, most recently in 2013. In addition to baseball games, Fenway Park has hosted football, soccer, and hockey games; concerts; and political events. In 2012, the park was listed in the National Register of Historic Places.

NIAGARA

NIAGARA FALLS, *Niagara Falls, New York*

Niagara Falls consists of three waterfalls along the border of the United States and Canada: the American Falls, the Canadian Falls, and the Bridal Veil Falls. The American Falls, pictured with the poem, range from 90 feet (27.4 meters) to 120 feet (36.6 meters) from the top of the falls to the rocks below. The falls were formed an estimated twelve thousand years ago. Today, millions of people visit each year to witness the falls' breathtaking beauty and hear their thunderous roar. The origin of the name Niagara is likely Mohawk since the first Europeans to see the falls were guided by Mohawks. In Mohawk, the root meaning of *throat-neck* is Oh-ni-ah-sa, which means "inside the neck," and may refer to the narrow flow of water between Lake Erie and Lake Ontario, which are connected by the falls. The first written version of Niagara appeared in 1641 as Onguiaahra, which has been translated as "Thunder of Waters."

SOURCES

"Bird Watching." Grand Canyon Chamber of Commerce. http://grandcanyoncvb.org/bird-watching/.

Boston Red Sox Attendance Data. Baseball Almanac. http://www.baseball-almanac.com/teams/rsoxatte.shtml.

Charlottin, François. "After 200 years, 125th still Harlem's 'main street.'" Columbia Daily Spectator, February 26, 2013. http://columbiaspectator.com/news/2013/02/26/after-200-years-125th-still-harlems-'main-street.

Cheng, Emma. "On 125th Street, a changing façade." Columbia Daily Spectator, February 27, 2013. http://columbiaspectator.com/news/2013/02/27/125th-street-changing-facade.

"Chinatown—Gateway Arch." Art and Architecture—San Francisco. http://www.artandarchitecture-sf.com/chinatown-san-francisco-may-11-2012.html.

Chinatown San Francisco. http://www.sanfranciscochinatown.com.

"Circus Museum." Visitor's brochure for The Ringling museum complex.

Denali: National Park & Preserve, Alaska. US National Park Service. http://www.nps.gov/dena/index.htm.

Di Ionno, Mark. "NJ's oldest lighthouse still burns brightly at Sandy Hook." NJ.com. http://www.nj.com/news/index.ssf/2014/06/njs_oldest_lighthouse_burning_bright_at_sandy_hook.html.

Elevations and Distances in the United States. US Geological Survey. http://egsc.usgs.gov/isb/pubs/booklets/elvadist/elvadist.html.

Facts about Niagara Falls. http://www.niagarafallslive.com/Facts_about_Niagara_Falls.htm.

Fenway Park. MLB.com. http://boston.redsox.mlb.com/bos/ballpark/.

Fernandez, Manny. "Fire Fells a Really Big Cowboy in Dallas." The New York Times, October 19, 2012. http://www.nytimes.com/2012/10/20/us/fire-destroys-big-tex-icon-of-texas-state-fair.html?_r=0.

Gateway: National Recreation Area, NY, NJ. US National Park Service. http://www.nps.gov/gate/historyculture/sandyhookmaritime.htm, and http://www.nps.gov/gate/historyculture/shlight250.htm.

Gerds, Warren. "Replica Iroquois longhouse predates Oneidas' move to Wisconsin." GreenBayPressGazette.com, August 19, 2009. http://archive.greenbaypressgazette.com/article/20090819/GPG04/908190581/Replica-Iroquois-longhouse-predates-Oneidas-move-Wisconsin.

Goldman, Marlene, and Jasmine J. Jopling. "San Francisco: Chinatown." SF Gate. http://www.sfgate.com/neighborhoods/sf/chinatown/.

Grand Canyon: National Park, Arizona. US National Park Service. http://www.nps.gov/grca/index.htm.

"History of the Circus Museum." The Ringling. http://www.ringling.org/history-circus-museum.

Hughes, Alan. "Looking Back . . . on the Meaning of 'Niagara.'" Newsletter of the Historical Society of St. Catharines, June 2010: 7–10. http://www.brocku.ca/webfm_send/31337.

Kimball, David. Venerable Relic: The Story of the Liberty Bell. Philadelphia, PA: Eastern National Park & Monument Association, 1989.

"Langston Hughes." Lawrence KS. http://www.visitlawrence.com/history/langston-hughes.

"Langston Hughes's hometown of Lawrence, KS." Poets.org. http://www.poets.org/poetsorg/listing/langston-hughess-hometown-lawrence-ks.

"The Liberty Bell." Independence: National Historical Park, Pennsylvania. US National Park Service. http://www.nps.gov/inde/historyculture/stories-libertybell.htm.

"Light List, volume 1: Atlantic Coast." US Department of Homeland Security, United States Coast Guard. http://www.navcen.uscg.gov/pdf/lightLists/LightList%20V1.pdf.

Miller, Bill. "Major League Ballparks: Largest to Smallest." The On Deck Circle: Baseball History, Commentary and Analysis. https://ondeckcircle.wordpress.com/2013/10/14/major-league-baseball-stadiums-largest-to-smallest/.

"Miniature Circus Finds Home at FSU's Ringling Museum." Florida State University, July 20, 2005. https://fsu.edu/news/2005/07/21/miniature.circus/.

Mississippi: National River & Recreation Area. US National Park Service. http://www.nps.gov/miss/index.htm.

Nash, Gary B. "Liberty Bell." The Encyclopedia of Greater Philadelphia. http://philadelphiaencyclopedia.org/archive/liberty-bell/.

National Museum of the American Indian. http://www.nmai.si.edu.

"Niagara Falls." World Waterfall Database. http://www.worldwaterfalldatabase.com/waterfall/Niagara-Falls-106/.

Niagara Falls State Park. http://www.niagarafallsstatepark.com.

"Oneidas Way of Life: Building Structures: Longhouses." Sovereign Oneida Nation of Wisconsin. http://www.oneidanation.org/culture/page.aspx?id=1308.

"River Facts." Mississippi River Resource Page. http://www.mississippiriverresource.com/River/RiverFacts.php.

"Rivers: North America." World Atlas. http://www.worldatlas.com/webimage/countrys/nariv2.htm.

"Sandy Hook, NJ." LighthouseFriends.com. http://www.lighthousefriends.com/light.asp?ID=378.

Sovereign Oneida Nation of Wisconsin. http://www.oneidanation.org/museum/longhouse.aspx.

"State Fair of Texas History." State Fair of Texas. http://bigtex.com/about/history/.

Watkins Museum of History. http://www.watkinsmuseum.org/exhibits/index.shtml.

UNITED S

CALIFORNIA

● Chinatown

Grand
Canyon
National
Park

ARIZONA

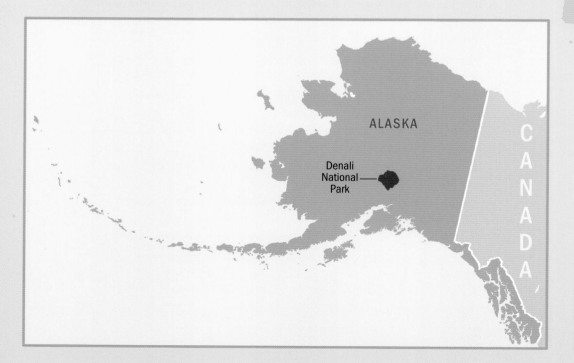

ALASKA

Denali
National
Park

CANADA

MEXICO

CANADA

TES

WISCONSIN

Oneida
Nation
Museum

Niagara
Falls

NEW
YORK

Fenway
Park

MASSACHUSETTS

PENNSYLVANIA

Harlem

Sandy Hook
Lighthouse

Liberty
Bell

NEW
JERSEY

WASHINGTON, DC

National
Museum of the
American Indian

KANSAS

Watkins
Museum
of History

Mississippi
River

State Fair
of Texas

MISSISSIPPI

FLORIDA

TEXAS

The Ringling
Circus Museum

N

W   E

S